Zoom!

and

Come Back, Mack!

By **Jenny Jinks**

Illustrated by **Ed Myer**

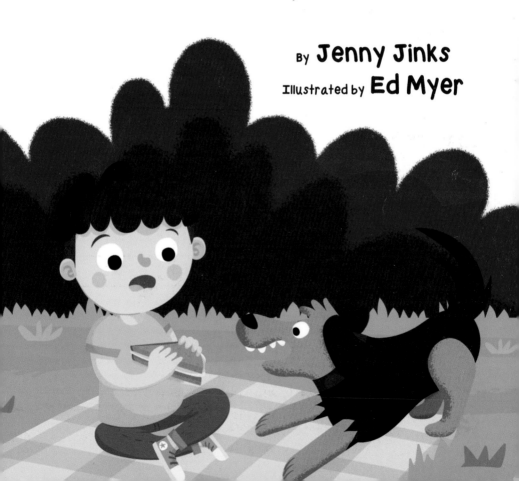

The Letter Z

Trace the lower and upper case letter with a finger. Sound out the letter.

Cross, down, cross

Cross, down, cross

Zoom!
and
Come Back, Mack!

'Zoom!' and 'Come Back, Mack!'
An original concept by Jenny Jinks
© Jenny Jinks

Illustrated by Ed Myer

Published by MAVERICK ARTS PUBLISHING LTD
Studio 3A, City Business Centre, 6 Brighton Road,
Horsham, West Sussex, RH13 5BB
© Maverick Arts Publishing Limited May 2018
+44 (0)1403 256941

A CIP catalogue record for this book is available at the British Library.

ISBN 978-1-84886-349-1

www.maverickbooks.co.uk

Red

This book is rated as: Red Band (Guided Reading)
This story is decodable at Letters and Sounds Phase 2.

Some words to familiarise:

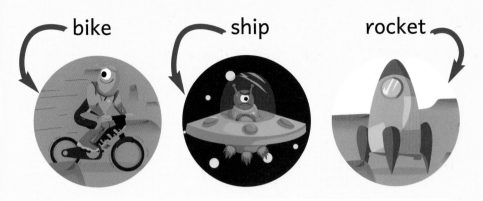

bike   ship   rocket

High-frequency words:

is off he his in on

Tips for Reading 'Zoom!'

- Practise the words listed above before reading the story.

- If the reader struggles with any of the other words, ask them to look for sounds they know in the word. Encourage them to sound out the words and help them read the words if necessary.

- After reading the story, ask the reader whether they remember the things that Zak was fast in.

Fun Activity

Can you think of any other things that are fast?

Zoom!

This is Zak. He is fast.

He runs off. Zoom!

Zak is fast on his bike.

He rushes off. Zoom!

Zak is fast in his van.

He zips off. Zoom!

Zak is fast in his ship.

He jets off. Zoom!

Zak is fast in his rocket.

He blasts off.
Zoom!

Zak is fast... asleep.

He nods off. Zzzzzzz.

The Letter M

Trace the lower and upper case letter with a finger. Sound out the letter.

*Down,
up,
around,
down,
up,
around,
down*

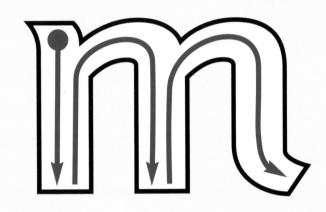

*Down,
up,
down,
up,
down*

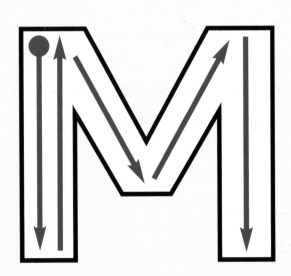

Some words to familiarise:

Mack   lunch   night

High-frequency words:

is   my   go   to   the   me

Tips for Reading 'Come Back, Mack!'

- Practise the words listed above before reading the story.

- If the reader struggles with any of the other words, ask them to look for sounds they know in the word. Encourage them to sound out the words and help them read the words if necessary.

- After reading the story, ask the reader if they remember what Mack took from the shop.

Fun Activity

Discuss why Mack might have been naughty.

Come Back, Mack!

This is my dog Mack.
Mack likes to come with me.

I go to the shop. Mack is with me.

I go to lunch. Mack is with me.

I go to the park. Mack is with me.

I go to bed.

Mack is not with me.

Book Bands for Guided Reading

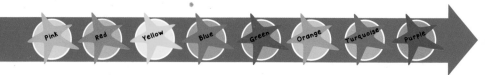

Red

Dog in a Dress and Run, Tom, Run!	Buzz and Jump! Jump!	Bam-Boo and I Wish	Sam the Star and Clown Fun!	Seeds and Stuck in the Tree
978-1-84886-290-6	978-1-84886-250-0	978-1-84886-251-7	978-1-84886-288-3	978-1-84886-289-0
Viv the Vet and Top Dog	Go Away! and Let's Make A Rocket	Catch It, Jess! and Cat Nap	Grandad's Cake and Grandad's Pat	Zoom! and Come Back, Mack!
978-1-84886-347-7	978-1-84886-350-7	978-1-84886-348-4	978-1-84886-351-4	978-1-84886-349-1

Plus many more titles in the scheme!

To view the whole Maverick Readers scheme, please visit:
www.maverickbooks.co.uk/early-readers

The Institute of Education book banding system is a scale of colours that reflects the various levels of reading difficulty. The bands are assigned by taking into account the content, the language style, the layout and phonics.

Maverick Early Readers are a bright, attractive range of books covering the pink to purple bands. All of these books have been book banded for guided reading to the industry standard and edited by a leading educational consultant.